Voyage to Shelter Cove

By Ralph da Costa Nunez

with Jesse Andrews Ellison

Illustrated by Madeline Gerstein Simon

White Tiger Press

New York

Introduction

Voyage to Shelter Cove is a fictional story of sea creatures who lose their homes on their reef and wander adrift and alone at sea. But this story also reflects the real lives of millions of people in this nation who are homeless today. Over one million of them are children, and it is they who are at greatest risk. The difficulties of not having a place to be with one's family, to sleep, to feel safe, and to study can be devastating. Children miss school, repeat grades, or drop out. But it doesn't have to be that way. Things can change, and *Voyage to Shelter Cove* is an important step in that process.

Today more than ever, homelessness is a children's issue, and the typical homeless person in America is a child. There is no better way to bring this message forward than through the hearts and minds of young children themselves. *Voyage to Shelter Cove* is an educational tool to help teach school-age children about homelessness, because the fact is that their peers have become the primary victims of this scourge. If we are ever going to end homelessness, the place to begin is with the youngest learners, who will use their knowledge to create a better world.

For over twenty years homelessness has been a family and children's issue, affecting one generation after another, with little change. At Homes for the Homeless, we understand that the time has come to transform the face of homelessness, to teach children through the misfortune, challenges, and hopes of sea creatures in *Voyage to Shelter Cove* what it is to lose your home, to live in a shelter, to find help, and to rebuild for the future. These are the basic lessons of homelessness that need to be told.

Voyage to Shelter Cove is the fourth in our educational series for children. As you read about Serena, Penelope, Pedro, and Herman, and the struggles they face after losing their homes, remember that children all over the country are facing the same situation at this very moment. Remember, it doesn't have to be that way. We can change it. And we will.

Leonard N. Stern
Founder/Chairman
Homes for the Homeless
New York City

One morning, deep, down under the sea,
a young seahorse named Serena was waking up.

It was a lovely morning.
Serena thought how lucky she was to live in such a safe and beautiful place.

Just then, she saw her neighbor Herman the hermit crab climbing along the coral.
He was wearing an old shell that had belonged to an oyster. "Good morning, Herman!" she called, "What a beautiful day!"

As usual, Herman grumbled back at her. "This darn sun is hurting my eyes. I've got to find a new shell. This one just doesn't fit right." Herman, like all hermit crabs, didn't grow his own shell. Instead he used other animals' old shells.

"Stop being such a crab," Serena said, giggling.

"Very funny," Herman said. "Serena, did you hear? Remember what happened to the reef next to ours? How the landlubbers built that giant pier and kicked everybody off the reef? Well, they're doing it here. People are coming in to build a fancy pier, and we'll all have to find new homes. Yup, there goes the neighborhood!"

Suddenly, Serena heard a
terrible sound, just like
thunder, but louder and more dangerous.
The sea got darker. The noise was
getting worse and worse. "See!" Herman
said, "They've started drilling!
Let's get out of here!"

Herman and Serena swam as
fast as they could away
from the reef.

The sea was full of coral dust, and it was getting darker and louder every minute.

Serena and Herman didn't even have time to go back to their little homes in the reef.

Looking back, they could see many others swimming away, too. Serena suddenly felt very afraid and very, very, far away from home. She tugged on Herman's claw. "Wait, wait. Let's rest for a minute."

They swam away from the group and drifted to the bottom of the sea. They tried to catch their breath.

Serena watched all the fish and creatures swim above her. She thought about all her friends and neighbors that she hadn't said goodbye to. She wondered whether she would ever see them again.

"Look, Serena!" said Herman. "Isn't that Penelope?"

They looked over to see their friend Penelope the parrot fish, panting and out of breath, a few feet away. "Penelope!" they shouted.

"Serena! Herman!" Penelope said. "Thank goodness I found you two!"

Serena looked around for Penelope's son. "Where's Pedro?" she asked.

Penelope pointed to a rock. "He was scared by all the noise. He's hiding behind that rock."

Serena saw a wide pair of eyes
peeking out from behind the
rock. She swam over. "Hi Pedro.
It's me, Serena. Don't be scared.
Herman, your mom, and I
are here with you."

Pedro nodded at her slowly
and swam out from behind the rock.

9

Serena looked at her three friends. Herman had lost his oyster shell and was shivering.

He looked silly without a shell, but he also looked scared. So did Penelope and Pedro. They were all very scared. They had lost their homes on the reef, and now they didn't have anywhere to live. They were homeless.

Herman must have realized how scared everyone was, too. Being the oldest, he decided to take charge. "OK," he said, "it's scary right now, but we'll make it through this. The most important thing is that the four of us stay together. We can help each other, right?"

"Right!" said Penelope, Pedro, and Serena.

"Good. First thing's first. We've got to find a new place to live," Herman said.
Serena knew it was dangerous for them in the ocean away from their reef.

None of them had ever been homeless before.
They didn't know how to survive in the
wide-open water on their own,
without a home.

Serena saw a light off in the distance. "Herman, why don't we go this way?"
"OK," Herman said, "Let's go." The four of them swam and swam.

Finally, Serena saw that the light was another coral reef.
"Look! Another reef! Maybe they'll let us stay there for the night?"

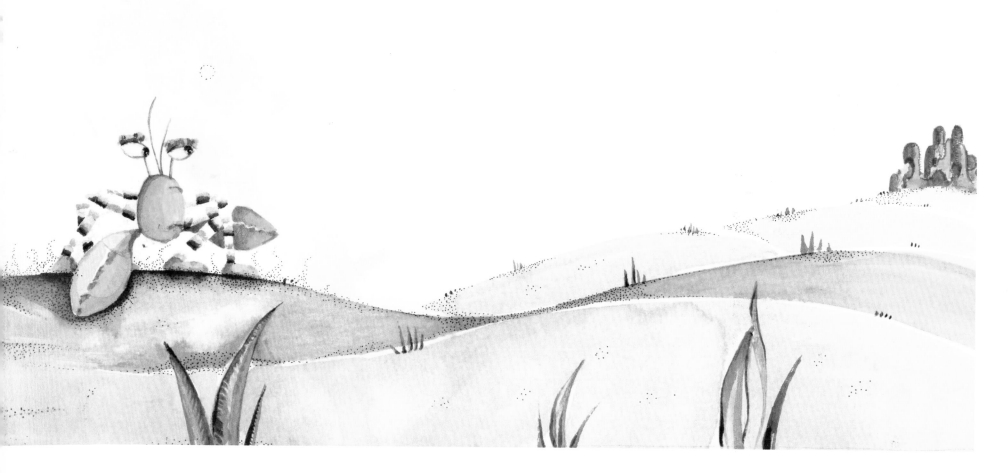

Soon they could see that the side of the reef was covered in red and orange sea flowers.

Pedro was usually very shy, but he started swimming closer and closer to the flowers.

He was so tired, and it looked like such a nice spot for a nap.

Suddenly, Serena spotted an eel ... then another ... and another! The sea floor was covered in them! Slippery, slimy eels slithered everywhere! Eels are the sneakiest creatures in the sea. They hide quietly in the algae and when fish and crabs are least expecting it, they sneak out and eat them up!

"Penelope! Eels!" Serena and Penelope started swimming after Pedro as quickly as they could.   They yelled, "Pedro!

Danger!

Stop swimming!"

Penelope finally caught up to Pedro.

She grabbed her son by his fin and pulled him away.

16

"That was close! We've got to keep looking out for each other. And don't talk to strange creatures alone!" warned Serena.

The four set off again looking for safer waters.

Serena was really beginning to worry.
What if none of the other coral reefs had room for them?
What if they couldn't find anywhere else to live?
What if they were homeless forever?
Serena was scared. She didn't like being homeless.

Serena, Penelope, Pedro, and Herman swam and swam until they came upon a little cove, tucked away from the busy open waters. Serena looked inside. She saw a big group of fish and sea animals swimming around. The four swam into the cove.

A big octopus came gliding over. "Hi! Let me guess. You're from the coral reef that was knocked down to make room for the big pier, right?" They nodded. "Well, you've come to the right place. Welcome to Shelter Cove, a place for everyone. My name is Oona. Most of the folks here call me Auntie Oona." She smiled at them.

"This is a bad time for everyone with so many reefs being torn down. More and more fish are becoming homeless every day," said Auntie Oona to her new friends.

"But you don't have to leave here until you're rested and ready." Auntie Oona showed them around Shelter Cove. Each of her eight giant arms was reaching down and helping with a class or project.

She was feeding a group of little starfish some sea kelp with one of her tentacles. "If you're hungry, you can get something to eat here, at The Algae Kitchen."

Then she pointed with another one of her arms. "Look, here are some seahorses working on their seaweed garden. They just won a prize for their sea cucumbers. They're also learning how to grow corals."

The group kept exploring the cove. "This here's our little school," said Auntie Oona. "See the starfish, crabs, and fish learning to read? Oh, and look over here. This family of angelfish is getting ready to move. They found a new home on another reef. They're not homeless anymore. Now each of you can pick an activity for yourself that will help you after you leave Shelter Cove."

Pedro didn't know how to read yet, so he joined the reading group at the little school.

Penelope went with him to see if she could help out.

Serena went to join the gardening class.

She wanted to learn how to grow new coral reefs for sea creatures to live in.

Herman decided to do arts and crafts.
He wanted to learn how to make his own shell.

gardening

gardening

arts & crafts

arts & crafts

Everyone was really busy with their classes at Shelter Cove. Sometimes, after dinner at The Algae Kitchen, Penelope, Pedro, Serena, and Herman got together to talk.

SEAWEED TEA

"I'm learning all about coral reefs and how they grow," said Serena. "Did you know that group of seahorses is planting a new reef not too far from here?"
"Well, I'm not going to need a new reef!" boasted Herman. "I'm almost done building my new shell. One that finally fits!"

"I'm going to miss Shelter Cove," said Pedro. "I really like it here."

"Me, too," said Serena, "especially Auntie Oona."

"Yes, she is really nice," said Herman. "And she does so much for everybody here."
They were all surprised to hear that.
Herman hardly ever said he liked anything! He was usually such a grump.

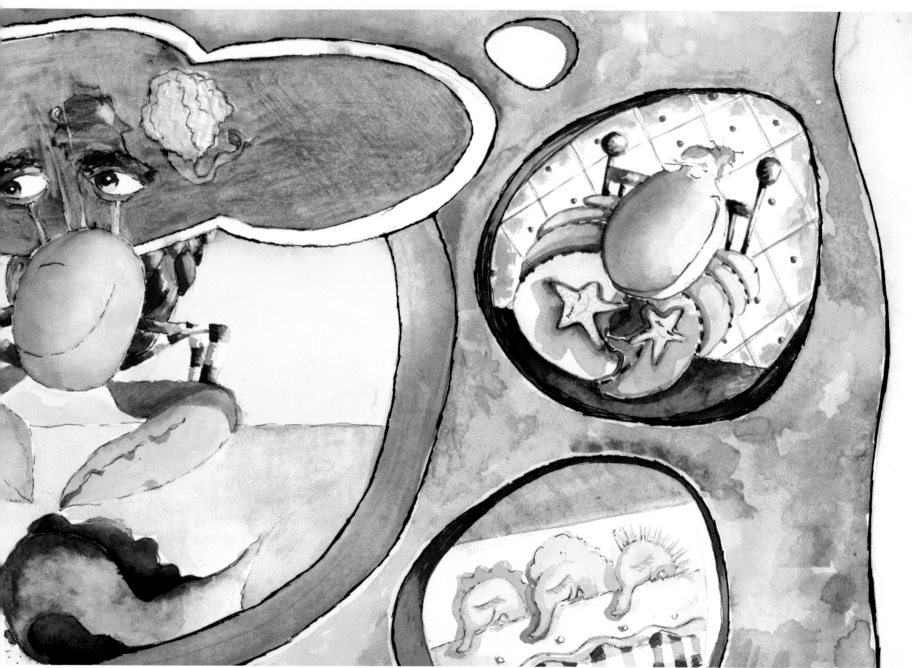

At Shelter Cove, Serena, Penelope, Pedro, and Herman met lots of other homeless fish and sea animals. Serena always tried to be very friendly to the new creatures. She remembered how scary it had been out in the ocean without a home.

27

After dinner one night, Auntie Oona told Serena, Penelope, Pedro, and Herman that soon they would be ready to leave Shelter Cove. "Where do you want to go after this?" she asked them.

"Pedro and I want to join a big school of fish," said Penelope. "I can become a real math teacher, and Pedro can keep studying."

"That's a great idea!" Auntie Oona said. "In school you will meet all sorts of other fish and learn lots of new things. What about you, Serena?"

"I want to go join the group of seahorses that are growing that new reef. That way, I can help other homeless sea creatures to have new homes and safe places to live. Did you know that there are thousands of homeless fish who need help? Well, there are! There are almost too many to count! I'm going to help them. What about you, Herman?"

"Actually," Auntie Oona said, "I'd like Herman to stay with me, if he doesn't mind. I need all the help I can get! Herman can help me show new folks around the cove and teach them to build their own beautiful shells. What do you say, Herman? Will you stay?"

Herman had never looked so happy! He blushed and nodded back at Auntie Oona, "Of course I'll stay! Here, I can help other crabs and seahorses and fish like us! With my new shell, I won't be homeless anymore, and I can help others find homes too."

"Well, I guess we're all going to go to different places, right, Serena?" Herman said.

"Yes, I guess so." Serena looked around at her friends.
She was sad that they were going to have to leave each other, but she was happy
that they had all found new homes. They had all come so far
since they got to Shelter Cove and had learned so many new things!

When it was time to leave, Auntie Oona and all the other creatures at Shelter Cove threw a big goodbye party. A group of starfish sang and danced for them. Pedro read a poem. Serena made a speech thanking everyone for their help. Everyone had a great time.

The next day, Serena said goodbye to Penelope, Pedro, and Herman. She promised to visit them soon. Even though she had felt very scared when she first came to Shelter Cove, Serena knew that she and her friends were stronger now. She was sad to leave the cove, but she was excited to start her new journey.

Voyage to Shelter Cove is the fourth in a series of children's book published by White Tiger Press. Each book addresses the issue of homelessness and poverty, and the approachable story lines make ideal points for discussion.

 Our Wish

 cooper's tale

 Saily's Journey

 VOYAGE TO SHELTER COVE

mango's quest

Read and collect all five!
Look for our series at your local library. All of our publications are available for purchase online at the Institute for Children and Poverty Web site, www.icpny.org.

Stories for children about homelessness

Home at Last

Home at Last is a collection of animated videos on family homelessness and poverty for grades K-5, based on the children's books by Ralph da Costa Nunez.

For bonus content, including a Learning Toolbox for educators, author interviews, activities and games, and ideas for helping in your community, or for more information on how to order, please go to: **www.icpny.org/HomeAtLast** or e-mail: **info@icpny.org**.